PARADISE TROUBLED

KATIE-ANNE MARTIN

Paradise Troubled
Published by Katie-Anne Martin
New Zealand

© 2020 Katie-Anne Martin

ISBN 978-0-473-51265-1 (Softcover)

Production & Typesetting:
Andrew Killick
Castle Publishing Services
www.castlepublishing.co.nz

Cover design:
Paul Smith

CHAPTER ONE

For the purposes of this story, we revisit the small fictitious town of Shackellby Downes. The year is 1988 and newlyweds Eden and Mark Hansen have just returned to the township from their honeymoon.

Eden had moved to join her husband in his large three-bedroomed villa which they had begun to renovate prior to becoming man and wife. The renovations now continued in earnest, with their friends assisting with the task whenever they had time. Eden's eye for detail was of much help, as the couple poured over paint charts and samples of material in order to choose fabric for new drapes and paint for the property. A handful of the couple's friends had gathered on one particular Saturday afternoon to attack the work still needing to be done.

They set to work sanding down windowsills and other furniture in preparation for painting and varnishing.

After several hours of tedious labour by those present, there was a knock at the front door. It was Dorothy Moore who had come to deliver a platter of her tasty homemade blueberry muffins. She was warmly welcomed as was the afternoon tea that she had provided.

Dorothy looked around. "You've made good progress," she said smiling.

"Yes," Mark replied with a grin. "Although the house looks a little bit like a shipwreck at the moment. These muffins smell wonderful," he said to Dorothy who smiled in reply, saying, "We couldn't have the workers starve now, could we?"

Everyone laughed.

Eden put the kettle on and it was not long before the group was sitting around in a comfortable silence sipping on well deserved cups of coffee and munching Dorothy's oven-fresh muffins.

Mark had taken three weeks leave of absence from his job as an electrician in order to complete the renovations on the house and was pleased with the progress made to date. The polished wooden floors in the villa were in good condition so he and Eden were concentrating on the painting of window sills as well as sanding other pieces of furniture in preparation for varnishing.

They had discussed the possibility of Eden securing employment now that they were married. However, because they wanted to begin a family straight away, it was decided that she would remain at home. They were preparing the back bedroom for their first child and both were eager for Eden to fall pregnant. Mark's wages were sufficient for him to care for his wife and their much anticipated first baby.

They were both grateful that Mark had chosen to learn a trade which had prepared him to gain a well paying job, working in a field that he enjoyed. His skills as an electrician came in handy around their home, as they did in the community at large, as there was no shortage of work for a qualified electrician.

The next two weeks seemed to crawl by, and the renovating work was relentless, but, finally, the last of the painting was finished and the new drapes hung neatly. Mark and Eden wandered through their home admiring their handiwork, both grateful that the work was finally complete.

"We deserve another holiday after all of this effort," Mark joked, and Eden groaned.

The renovating work had certainly been a hard grind but now they could enjoy the fruits of their labour.

"Let's go out for dinner tonight," Eden suggested, to which Mark replied, "A brilliant idea, sweetheart. It seems like we haven't stopped for much of a break since the honeymoon, nor spent any real quality time together."

Eden wore a soft blue strapless dress for her evening out with Mark.

Sitting opposite one another at the restaurant, they studied the menu. Looking up suddenly, Eden caught Mark gazing at the scars on her neck and shoulders with tears in his eyes.

She asked with some anxiety if her scarring made her less attractive to him.

"Of course not, my sweetheart," Mark replied tenderly. "I was just reflecting upon all of the suffering that you have endured – that we both endured before you finally became mine to have and to hold forevermore." He added, "I have the most beautiful wife in the whole world and I thank our God every day for you, my precious and stunning bride."

Eden relaxed as tears filled her eyes also. She paused

before smiling, and taking her husband's hand, she softly replied, "I, too, thank God for you, my darling. I really couldn't be happier." Eden continued to speak. "Isn't it incredible the way that God finally brought us together?" she mused, and Mark agreed.

"When you left town," he said, "I honestly didn't think that I had any hope of ever seeing you again, and that meant, at that time, life for me was over." He added, "If I couldn't have you, I didn't want anyone."

"I am so sorry," Eden whispered to Mark. "I hurt you so very dreadfully – much more than I realized at the time." She continued to speak. "When I got burned, I truly believed that I had become 'damaged goods' and that you wouldn't want me anymore – that the best decision to make was to cut you out of my life. I thought that after some time had passed, you would fall in love again and forget about me. I honestly believed that I was doing you a favour."

Eden continued. "Also, at that time, I was quite a vulnerable and messed up young lady with many issues of my own."

She began to talk about her growing up years. "As a teenager, with my alcoholic father dependent on me to care for him, I felt as though I'd lost control of my life – of who I was. That is why I turned to starving myself when I was just sixteen years old. I felt that if I looked good on the outside, then I would gain the acceptance and love I craved from other people. I was convinced that this was the only way in which I would be able to successfully navigate my way through life. I practised relentlessly in order to cover my anxieties and fears. After falling in love with you, I thought that finally I'd be happy. However, the horrific burns were the last straw, and at that time I, too, gave up on life in lots of ways, thinking that my disfigurement would turn even you away. I believed that I had lost all chance of happiness, and began to punish myself."

By this time, both Eden and Mark were becoming a little emotional. Eden nervously looked around her as the restaurant began to fill up with people. Mark leaned over and whispered into her ear.

"What say we leave dining out here for another night, and instead pick up some take-outs which we can eat in private – somewhere where I can show you how passionately I love you. We don't need crowds around us tonight, my gorgeous woman."

A thankful Eden agreed and after cancelling their table at the restaurant, Mark took his wife's arm and guided her out to their car. "How does a seafood dinner for two at our place sound?" he asked.

Eden nodded her head vigorously and leaned up to kiss Mark on the cheek. "Sounds good to me," she said, "and with the best company one could wish for," she stated.

Over a delicious dinner, Eden continued to share with Mark the painful things that were in her heart – experiences from her past which she had never spoken of in depth to anyone.

She spoke of the loneliness she felt at having been pulled out of school to care for her father who had become a very self absorbed person once the alcohol had begun to grip him. "I had lost control over so much of my life." She wept as she sat with her husband on the couch in their lounge. "The only thing I felt that I had control over at such a young age, was what I ate," Eden continued, Mark drew her close, silently comforting his wife as she continued to open up to him. "I felt that I had to be strong for my Dad," Eden said as she reflected on those painful times. "But there was no-one to whom I could turn. I missed my mother so badly that it seemed to be almost a physical pain," she whispered before burying her head on Mark's shoulder and giving full vent to her sorrow.

As her tears fell, Mark became emotional too, as his heart overflowed with compassion for the woman he loved. Finally, with her tears spent, an exhausted Eden fell asleep still leaning against Mark who gently stroked her hair as she leaned against his chest. He quietly thanked the God Who had blessed his life with this beautiful treasure of a wife.

CHAPTER TWO

When Mark returned to work, Eden set out to be the perfect housewife. She kept their home spotless, as well as regularly thumbing through an array of recipe books in order to find new and exciting dishes with which to treat her husband for dinner at night. She also spent a lot of time visiting Dorothy Moore to whom she had been very close for years. Dorothy enjoyed her visits from Eden who would chatter away about all kinds of things over mugs of hot coffee and homemade muffins which were always plentiful at Dorothy's house. Dorothy would sit and listen to Eden, enjoying the younger woman's enthusiasm for life, and especially her passion for the God Whom they both loved and served.

It hadn't taken Eden long after having married Mark to discover that he was a sleep walker. On a regular basis he had got up in the night and, while fast asleep, had walked around their house. Eden found this to be amusing, as whenever she mentioned to her husband that he had been sleep walking, he had disbelieved her, making a joke of it by telling her that he must have been looking for her.

"See how much I love you?" he smiled. "I even search for you while I'm asleep."

However, he refused to believe that he sleep walked, while many a night, Eden quietly followed him while he opened cupboard doors and did other strange things while asleep in the night hours.

One morning, while visiting with her older friend, Eden confided in Dorothy, telling her that she and Mark were hoping for a baby as soon as possible.

"Mark's great with children and would make a good father," she said.

Dorothy was delighted for the couple, telling Eden that she would make a good mother as well.

The two then sat for a while in a comfortable silence, each caught up in her individual thoughts.

Dorothy, having married later in life, had not had the chance to become a mother and she was glad that Eden and Mark were wanting to start a family early in their marriage.

Eden glanced at her watch and got quickly to her feet, telling Dorothy that she needed to leave as she was meeting her cousin, Vicky Morgan, for lunch in town that day. Time often slipped by quickly when Eden was visiting Dorothy as they were very fond of one another, and had much in common. In fact, Dorothy, soon after having met Eden, had begun to view her as a daughter and Eden, in response, viewed the older woman as the mother figure she had hungered for during much of her life, having lost her own mother at the tender age of just eleven years old.

Eden met Vicky outside the bank in which her cousin

worked as a teller in town, and the two young women walked to a coffee shop where, having bought their lunch, they sat down at one of the tables outside.

Vicky was having trouble with one of her senior co-workers at the bank. She was a new head teller who had seemed to have taken a dislike to Vicky and was endeavouring to stir up trouble for her.

Eden sympathized with her cousin, agreeing that there was no room for bullying in the work place.

Vicky grimaced, telling Eden that this woman seemed to have taken exception to the fact that Vicky was a follower of Christ, and was making things difficult for her.

Vicky studied her cousin for a moment, then told Eden that she looked content. "Married life must be suiting you," she said.

Eden smiled in reply and confided in Vicky that she and Mark were keen to start a family.

Vicky made a face and replied, "Rather you than me. I would absolutely loath having my sleep interrupted by a baby, and changing nappies would be an absolute nightmare," she replied.

Eden grinned, and told Vicky that having been an only child herself she wanted a large family, to which Vicky said nothing. The young women finished their coffee in a comfortable silence, then Vicky finally stood up, telling Eden that she had better get back to work.

After the cousins had said their goodbyes, Eden decided to do some window shopping to fill in a little bit of time before returning home to prepare Mark's dinner. She was feeling a little bored and decided to call into the Centre on her way home to see if they needed her help with anything.

That evening over dinner, she discussed with Mark the possibility of finding some paid employment for a while, because she hadn't fallen pregnant immediately as the couple had hoped.

Mark looked at her and asked if she felt up to working after all that she had been through in the last six or so years. "Oh, yes," Eden replied. "I feel as though I am going crazy trying to fill in my days while you are at work. I'm more than ready to get a job."

"Well, then," Mark replied, "I guess it wouldn't hurt for you to look into it then."

"Great!" Eden replied enthusiastically. "I will do some door knocking then," she said. "I would ideally like to work in a florist shop, as that is where my talents lie," she said. "However, with only two florists in town, it's unlikely that they will need staff."

Mark replied, "It won't hurt to enquire, honey," and Eden agreed, making up her mind to do so the following day.

As expected, both of the town's florist shops were fully staffed but Eden secured part time work in the town's library, although this was not her first choice. Eden was grateful for the job, which she was to begin the following week.

Eden was an avid reader, and began to enjoy her new job, settling into the position easily, as well as quickly getting to know and enjoy the company of her workmates. However, as time passed, she and Mark were becoming a little concerned as to why she was failing to become pregnant. They decided that it wouldn't hurt for them both to get themselves checked out by their local doctor just to make sure that all was in order in that area, and consequently made an appointment for just under a week's time.

It was an anxious wait for both Eden and Mark. However, the day of the doctor's visit finally arrived.

Doctor Jenky was a tall, slightly built woman who appeared to be in her mid fifties. She was dressed immaculately, with her long hair, which was peppered with grey, pulled up in a bun, which sat at the back of her head accentuating her sharp features. With the barest hint of a smile, she asked Mark and Eden to take a seat in the two semi comfortable chairs in front of the desk in her office.

The couple did not know this doctor very well as she had only recently moved to the Downes. This increased their nervousness.

Due to the fact that Eden was obviously underweight for her height, the physician began by asking her some questions about her menstrual bleeding which Eden admitted was unusually light.

After having given the young woman a physical and pelvic examination, she ordered that a blood test be carried out on Eden. Also, a sperm sample was requested from Mark. The couple were then advised to try not to worry while awaiting the results of the tests. A follow up appointment was made for them, in a fortnight's time in order to provide time for the tests to be analyzed.

Eden and Mark were a little nervous but were hopeful that neither of them was infertile and that it would be just a matter of time before Eden fell pregnant. However, they spent much time in prayer concerning this matter over the following couple of weeks.

Time seemed to drag for Eden and Mark as they navigated the fortnight, with the impending doctor's consultation forefront in the minds of both of them. Eden found it difficult to concentrate on her work at the library while, at the same time, finding it a welcome distraction.

Mark endeavoured to speak words of encouragement to his wife, while also experiencing some anxiety as to what the test results might possibly reveal.

The couple both desperately wanted a family. Eden, in particular, was eager to become a mum. Having been the only child of her own parents, she was hoping for at least four children.

She spoke to Dorothy Moore with some anxiety concerning the upcoming follow up doctor's appointment. Dorothy told her younger friend that her worries might all be for nothing and suggested that Eden think positively in the meantime, telling her that there was nothing that she and Mark could do until they visited with the doctor again.

"Don't torture yourself with 'ifs' and 'maybe's,' she counselled Eden.

She promised also to pray for the couple as they awaited the results of the tests.

"Take it one day at a time, dear," she advised Eden, as she offered her some freshly baked muffins and a freshly brewed cup of coffee. The two women sat in silence as they consumed their coffee and muffins.

CHAPTER THREE

Mark and Eden sat in Doctor Jenky's waiting room, waiting to be called into her office for their all important appointment. They sat together in silence, both preoccupied with their individual thoughts as they wondered how the visit would go. After what seemed to be an impossibly long time, the doctor appeared and ushered the couple into her office, inviting them to be seated.

She rustled some papers in her hand as she leaned across her desk to speak. She addressed Eden.

"It is possible that you are experiencing ovulation problems," she said to the young lady.

"Wh-what do you mean?" Eden stuttered.

The doctor responded calmly. "We need to do a little more testing in order to make a certain diagnosis. Firstly, I will need a urine sample from you," the doctor stated. "Are you able to do that for me now?" she asked.

Eden replied that she would and made her way to the bathroom to produce the sample requested.

When she returned, the physician continued to speak. "I will need to refer you to a fertility specialist in the city in order to confirm the diagnosis, and for you to talk to her about treatment options."

She then said that she would make an appointment and that Eden would hopefully receive an appointment card in the mail within the next few weeks.

The doctor smiled before standing to her feet to indicate that the appointment was over.

Doctor Jenky gently touched an anxious Eden on the shoulder, reiterating that there were ways to treat her condition which had been used with some success on other women. She also told the couple to try not to worry unduly. She advised Eden to do her best to increase her weight, telling her that this might be a helpful addition to the treatment she might receive from the specialist.

Eden walked slowly and silently with Mark to their car following their appointment. Mark placed his arm around his wife's shoulder, sensing that she was extremely unsettled at the doctor's report. He kissed her gently on the top of her head as they entered their vehicle. Once inside the car, the young woman broke down, sobbing uncontrollably as Mark held her and stroked her hair.

"Mark," she choked out her words. "I cannot even give you a baby. I feel so useless."

Mark spoke softly to his bride as tears of love for her filled his own eyes. "Sweetheart," he said gently, "you are by far the most important person in my life – more important than any baby could be. I couldn't live a day without you in my life," he continued to speak. "We will work through this together."

He reminded Eden that there was the hope of treatment

for her condition and stated that after having lost Eden for so many years before they had married, he was deliriously happy to have her as his precious wife regardless of whether or not their lives together were to include children. Mark then silently drove to the little reserve which had become so special to the couple and, getting out of the car, he took his wife's arm and they walked. Eden was still visibly upset and Mark endeavoured to reassure and encourage her. "This isn't your fault, darling," he whispered as he pushed back her glossy curls to kiss the tip of her ear. "You are more precious to me than anything," he spoke softly to her. However, Eden refused to be comforted and continued to berate herself as they walked through the reserve. Mark drew his wife close and quietly cuddled her as she continued to give expression to her pent up emotions.

Mark was also a bit shattered by the doctor's report but was mainly concerned for Eden as he knew how desperately she wanted to have a family. He also wanted to have children. However, this was not as important to him as it was to his wife. The two prayed together before bed that night asking that God would provide for the treatment that Eden was to receive to be successful. Doctor Jenky had told them that it was successful for an average of forty percent of the women to whom it was administered. There were also some possible side effects to consider. The questions swirled in both Eden's and Mark's minds as they climbed into bed that evening and both attempted to obtain some sleep.

The following morning, Eden was a little withdrawn. Both Mark and she had not slept well, and although Mark endeavoured to cheer his wife up while they sat at the kitchen table together eating breakfast, Eden barely responded. After Mark had left for work, Eden, having some time before she was due at the library, decided to drive herself to town and do some window shopping.

She didn't feel as though she wanted to communicate with anyone and thought that to browse in the windows of some of the shops would be therapeutic for her, as she had much on her mind following yesterday's doctor's appointment. The news that she and Mark had been given had come as a shock to both of them, and Eden simply wanted some time out in order to digest the information that Dr Jenky had given them.

The City Centre was quite busy that morning, and Eden decided to have a seat in the mall for a time first. She felt that in some way she had been created as less than a woman because of the issues she was experiencing which prevented Mark and herself having a baby. Of course, this was untrue.

However, Eden was very much a perfectionist and blamed herself quite unjustly for these problems, as she did with many of the mostly minor problems which she and Mark encountered in general, from time to time, as husband and wife. She was extremely frustrated with herself, coming to the conclusion (as she often did) that she was 'damaged goods' and had let her husband down concerning this very sensitive area of childbearing. The feelings of self hatred, combined with the insecurity of many years ago rising up in her, brought tears to her eyes which she furiously wiped away.

Old voices from the past whispered into her ears. "You're not good enough. You are useless," they taunted her. Eden shook her head in an effort to distance herself from them.

Finally, she rose to her feet and, hoping that she wouldn't cross paths with anyone who wanted to talk to her, walked over to a chemist shop and spent some time smelling the different perfumes and soaps for sale on the shelves. Then, on a whim, she walked quickly to a florist store where she impulsively purchased for herself a bunch of pink carnations. Carnations were her favourite type of flower as they reminded her of her mother who had passed on to Eden her particular love of them, while Eden was still just a child.

As she inhaled the aroma of the beautifully presented flowers, Eden began to feel considerably more positive in mood. She decided to drive to Dorothy Moore's home for a brief visit as she had an hour or so to fill before she was due to begin work at the library. Dorothy welcomed her and inquired as to how the doctor's appointment had gone for her and Mark. Immediately, Eden's face fell and she replied that she would talk to Dorothy about it some other time.

Sitting in a comfortable chair in Dorothy's lounge, she asked her older friend how she was.

Although sensing that all was not well, and feeling concerned, Dorothy wisely did not pursue the topic of Eden's visit with the clinician, and the two kept their conversation superficial and reasonably lighthearted. Eden told Dorothy that she would visit in a day or so to talk to her about the results of her doctor's appointment. Dorothy nodded and told the young woman to take all the time she needed before sharing the outcome with her.

Eden went to work that afternoon, grateful for her job. Even though she would have enjoyed working in one of the town's two florist shops, she was grateful for the distraction provided her by her library job. The afternoon seemed to go quickly for her that day and she arrived home about 4pm and began to prepare dinner. Mark arrived home about an hour later and he placed some small tins of liquid food supplement onto the kitchen bench. Eden looked at him questioningly and after kissing her, he explained that he had bought some food supplements for her because the doctor had advised her to gain some weight.

"Thank you, sweetheart," Eden responded as she looked a little more closely at the tins of liquid nutrition. Reading the instructions, she remarked to her husband that they were supposed to be consumed with meals.

"I don't know that I can manage to drink these as well as to eat dinner," she stated.

Mark looked a bit deflated so she quickly added that she would do her best to consume them.

Mark smiled and reminded his wife that he had only bought them because he wanted them to have the best possible chance of having at least one child. "For your sake more than mine," he told her.

Eden smiled at her husband's sweet and caring nature, and affectionately ruffled his hair.

CHAPTER FOUR

It was to be Mark's 30th birthday in under a month's time and Eden decided to throw a surprise party for him. With a reasonable amount of time to plan for it, she decided that she would enlist the help of Christine Brewer, as well as Dorothy, to organise it when the time grew closer. Eden was anticipating holding the birthday bash at the Centre. She smiled as she thought of the joy that it would bring to Mark who had been particularly supportive of Eden lately concerning her possible inability to give him a child. After all, Mark also wanted a family and had instead devoted much time to consoling his wife rather than voicing his own frustrations over this issue.

To the surprise of the couple, they received a phone call a few days later from West End City Hospital's Fertility Department to ask if Eden was able to attend an appointment with a Doctor Susan Mills as they had received a cancellation and consequently had a spare appointment slot.

Eden and Mark were relieved and somewhat excited as they had been expecting to wait much longer for this appointment which was now set down for just eight days time at 1.30pm.

Eden decided to visit with Dorothy Moore the following

morning before work in order to explain to the older woman all that had taken place over the preceding two or so weeks. She was feeling a little more positive in mood and she was also aware that Dorothy was concerned for her following their last visit together. She felt a sense of guilt for not confiding in Dorothy at an earlier time.

Dorothy sat quietly as Eden told her about the outcome of her and Mark's second appointment with Doctor Jenky. The younger woman was a little emotional as she expressed her concerns about her possible inability to give Mark a family, which was something that she, too, wanted desperately. Finally, with tears in her own eyes, Dorothy spoke, telling Eden to remember that their options were far from exhausted. She advised her friend to take things one step at a time and promised to pray for the couple concerning their upcoming appointment with the specialist at West End.

"You were fortunate to obtain an appointment so quickly," she remarked as she rubbed Eden's shoulders. Dorothy then wrapped her arms around her friend in an attempt to comfort and to encourage her. Eden broke down, sobbing as she clung to Dorothy who just held her.

Finally, Eden wiped her eyes and blew her nose, telling Dorothy that a good cry was what she had been needing and that she felt better for it. Dorothy smiled and patted Eden on the shoulder before fixing a cup of coffee and a freshly buttered muffin for each of them. They sat in a relaxed silence as they enjoyed their morning tea. Eden promised to keep the older lady updated and she then left to prepare for work at the library that afternoon.

The Library was usually a quiet and orderly place in which to work. However, to her great dismay, when Eden entered the building to begin work that particular afternoon, she was greeted by the loud and high pitched voice of Veronica Hartly. She was airing her views in no uncertain terms and holding a book which she was waving in the air. Speaking to Jennifer Lee, the poor lady at the desk whom she had bailed up, Mrs Hartly was complaining about a perceived lack of 'good taste' in one of the books she had borrowed. Veronica was waving the book around in the air as, spitting and spluttering, she vented her anger at Jennifer Lee who was on duty at reception that afternoon. Jennifer was clearly embarrassed by Veronica's outburst which was aimed at the library workers in general.

"I tell you," Veronica spoke at fever pitch. "This library used to be a respectable place. I was appalled to read the words, 'sexual intercourse,' in this book. In my day," she continued to berate the unfortunate librarian, "reading was a pleasure and there was never any inappropriate content in the books from this library. I demand that this book be removed immediately from the shelves!"

Veronica pursed her thin lips and, with her hands on her hips, she glared at the lady she was addressing. Jennifer did her best to placate the loud-mouthed woman in front of her, explaining to Veronica that the book which she was complaining about was an educational manual on marriage which had been written for teenagers.

However, seemingly deaf to the librarian's words, Veronica continued with her barrage of abuse until Jennifer firmly instructed the loud-mouthed woman to leave the building as she was disturbing the other people there. A flushed and furious Veronica responded by slamming the book onto the counter, and looking around as she turned to leave, stated that she would never set foot in a library such as this again. Then, with a haughty shake of the head, she tottered out of the Library and down the steps still muttering in her anger and distress about the book in question.

A stunned Eden stared open-mouthed at Jennifer before they both burst into laughter.

"My goodness!" Jennifer stated, "That woman is a walking disaster."

Bent double with laughter by this time, Eden just looked at her co-worker unable to respond.

Finally, the two endeavoured to compose themselves. Fortunately, there were only a few people in the library at the time, but each of them had paused to listen with more than a little amusement to Veronica's loud verbal outburst, attempting to contain their laughter as the scene had unfolded, while feeling pity for the hapless Jennifer whom they all knew and respected. This was certainly an interesting beginning to Eden's afternoon's work at the library, and she wondered why Veronica had borrowed a manual for marriage, the thought of which caused her to erupt again in a fit of giggles.

The rest of the afternoon was uneventful and Eden left after work, stopping on her way home to pick up some groceries. She wondered what to cook Mark and herself for dinner that evening.

Something simple, she decided as she put her supermarket shopping away.

The rest of the week passed quickly for Eden as well as for Mark who was busy at work.

Almost before they knew it, the day for Eden's appointment at the City Hospital arrived, and the couple were rushing to get ready.

Mark and Eden had taken the day off work, and they drove via the North bound motorway to West End City Hospital to visit with Doctor Mills. The couple were quiet throughout the trip and arrived at the hospital at 1.15pm, with just a quarter of an hour to spare before Eden's appointment.

Having located the fertility clinic, they walked over to reception, advising the nurse behind the desk that they had arrived, handing her the appointment card.

With a smile and a cheerful "Good afternoon!" the nurse proceeded to ask a series of questions of Eden, including her date of birth. She then directed the couple to wait in a room telling them that the specialist would be with them shortly. An anxious Eden drew in a long breath. She and Mark thanked the nurse and sat in a couple of hard-backed chairs in the clinic's waiting room.

There were several other women in the waiting room. All were sitting quietly. Mark squeezed Eden's hand in an attempt to encourage her, although he, too, was a little unsettled.

It was about twenty minutes before Eden's name was called and the couple were led to a spacious office which contained a clinical white bed with a rather dull grey curtain partially pulled around it.

Hand in hand, they sat in front of the doctor's desk as they waited for her to arrive. The nurse returned with a thin file in her hand. She placed this on the desk before leaving the room again.

Eden shivered slightly and glanced at Mark who was staring at the ground and seemed to be lost in his thoughts.

A few minutes later, Doctor Mills entered the room. She was a short lady with prominent teeth and fair coloured hair. She looked to be in her mid to late forties, and wore a white coat, with a stethoscope hanging around her neck. She greeted the couple, introducing herself as Susan Mills.

"And you are Eden Hansen?" she enquired looking at Eden, who replied that, yes, she was Eden, and gesturing towards Mark, informed the doctor that he was her husband. The doctor sat at the desk and opened the file.

After checking Eden's date of birth, she sat reading the paperwork in the file quietly for a few minutes. She finally looked up and addressed Eden, telling her that her test results had come back, and that she had received a detailed report from the doctor who had referred her.

"I would like to do a pelvic examination. Is that all right?" she asked Eden, who gave her consent.

Susan Mills stood to her feet, telling the couple that she would return shortly to carry out the examination before leaving the office.

A nurse entered and weighed Eden as well as taking her temperature and blood pressure before handing her a cream-coloured cuddly rug and asking her to remove her clothing from the waist down and to lay on the bed with the blanket to cover herself. The nurse then left the room, and Eden complied with the instructions given her, pulling the curtain around the cubicle and waiting quietly on the bed for the doctor to return.

Doctor Mills entered the room and carried out the examination on her patient. She then left Eden to get into her clothes and to join her and Mark who was still sitting in front of the desk.

The doctor looked at Eden and began to speak to her. "I have diagnosed you with a condition called Polycystic Ovarian Syndrome," she told Eden, who glanced at Mark before turning back to the doctor who explained to Eden that she was not ovulating regularly and that this was the cause of her infertility struggles. "I can offer you some treatment which has had a degree of success in helping with this problem" she stated.

Eden and Mark waited for the doctor to continue speaking. "I propose to prescribe an oral medication for you which might help," she explained. "The name of the medication is Clomiphane Citrate." She handed Eden a booklet which would explain to the couple how this medication worked. It also contained instructions for taking the pills if Eden and Mark agreed to the treatment which the doctor stated was recommended for those with Eden's diagnosis.

She would need to take a course of this medication and, if need be, several short courses could be prescribed. "This medication will often cause ovulation to take place," she explained.

"What about side effects?" Mark asked.

"There are some side effects," Doctor Mills replied. "However, these can often be minimal," she told the couple.

Turning to Eden, she continued to speak. "You might get a bit of an upset stomach, maybe some dizziness. Also, headaches can be side effects, as well as breast tenderness and nausea. You can read more fully about this treatment in the booklet I have given you. However," she continued, "if you experience side effects which become troubling, you can contact myself or your local doctor.

The side effects are also explained in greater detail in the booklet which I have given you. She stood to her feet to indicate that the appointment was finished and told the couple to take some time to study the booklet and to decide if Eden wanted to go ahead with the treatment. She made an appointment to see them again in a fortnight, at which time the treatment would be started if Eden was happy to proceed with it.

CHAPTER FIVE

Eden began to prepare for the surprise birthday party that she was going to throw for Mark. His birthday was to be on June 8th so she now had just eighteen days in which to organize it.

Going into town the following morning, she purchased some sheets of thin cream and gold cardboard which she intended to cut up and make invitations to send to Mark's friends and family.

She was hoping that his parents would be able to travel into the Downes to join the birthday celebrations. Eden also began to make a detailed list of all that she would need in order for Mark's party to be the very best one possible. She realized that she needed a lot of bits and pieces for the party to be perfect. One thing to consider was the birthday cake which she decided to have professionally made as baking was really not her forte. She carefully concealed the things that she was gathering from Mark as she wanted his birthday bash to be a complete surprise for him. She had decided to make the birthday celebration a pot luck tea which meant that each guest would contribute a meal suitable for dinner. The food would be shared amongst those who attended the party.

Both Eden and Mark were considerably more settled, as, after having carefully read through the booklet given them by Doctor Mills, they had decided upon the answer that they would give her at the impending appointment concerning treatment for Eden.

Eden phoned a bakery in the city to order a birthday cake for Mark, explaining exactly how she wanted it to be made and decorated. She told the lady at the Cookies and Cakes Bakehouse that she would call in to pay a deposit on the cake in about a week's time and asked if they would be able to create the type of cake that she had specified. "Yes, we can do that for you," she was told and she hung up the phone with a smile as she thought about how much she hoped that Mark would enjoy his party in general.

She also phoned Mike Brewer in order to book the Centre for the big night. He promised to gather some people to help with the decorations.

The following day, having hand written the invitations, Eden delivered them. This took a considerable amount of time.

She then called in on Dorothy Moore telling her about the proposed party and handing her an invitation.

"My goodness!" Dorothy remarked. "You have been busy, my dear," Eden replied that she hoped that the party would be a success and that Mark would enjoy it along with his friends.

Dorothy said that she was sure it would be a fantastic evening, telling Eden that it was a lovely idea.

Eden then updated the older lady on her recent appointment with the doctor at West End, also telling her what Mark and she had decided to do. Dorothy was pleased to see her happier and she commented on Eden's relaxed manner.

"Oh, yes, I am more settled," Eden replied. "We both are, now that we've made a decision regarding the treatment which has been offered us."

She smiled at Dorothy, then asked how life had been going for her. Dorothy replied that she couldn't complain and that she had been assisting with some chores at the Centre lately.

"They are thinking of painting it," she told Eden.

Then she said that she had missed Eden's visits lately, although she understood that the young woman had been attending to lots of things in recent times. Eden replied that she surely had, but that she would make an effort to visit Dorothy more often now that some of her big issues had been dealt with.

Three days later, with Mark once again taking the day off work, he and Eden drove to West End City Hospital to attend their second appointment with the fertility specialist. Both were very much more relaxed now that they had made their decision concerning Eden's fertility treatment.

Doctor Mills welcomed them and asked if the couple had reached a decision.

Eden replied in the affirmative. "I want to begin treatment, please," she stated.

The doctor smiled and told the couple that she would write out a prescription which would need to be filled at the hospital's pharmacy. She asked Eden whether she was clear on when to start taking the medication as well as on the regime in general.

"Yes," Eden replied. "The booklet explained it perfectly."

"Great!" Doctor Mills responded before handing her the prescription. "Begin by taking one pill two days after menstruation begins and continue to take one tablet daily for a total of five days. We are hoping that you will ovulate between five and ten days after you finish the five day course of Clomiphene Citrate. If that fails to happen, we can prescribe a second course with a stronger dose."

Eden nodded to show that she understood and the doctor spoke again. "Don't forget to contact myself, or your local doctor, if you experience troubling side effects," she told Eden. "Further prescriptions, should you need them, can be accessed through your local medical practitioner," she told the young lady, "including blood tests to determine if you fall pregnant," she added.

Wishing the couple good luck, she smiled as she stood to usher Eden and Mark out.

After locating the hospital's pharmacy, they drove home with the bottle of medication which had been prescribed for them. Eden was due to begin menstruation, so she and Mark waited with anticipation for this to occur.

Four days later, Eden was able to take the first dose of her fertility medication. She waited anxiously for the Clomiphene Citrate to get into her system, wondering how bad the side effects would be for her, as well as hoping that the pills would do their work well so that she might conceive. She desperately wanted to be among those for whom the treatment had been successful.

As Mark's birthday approached, Eden began to consider

what she might buy him as gifts for his big day. He desperately needed some new clothing so that was on the list. She went into one of the menswear stores in the town's main street and purchased a straight-legged pair of black jeans as well as several casual, yet nice, shirts. Blue was a colour which she thought particularly suited Mark, so one of the shirts she bought him was blue and white striped. Aftershave was included in the birthday shopping, as was shower gel and a hair shampoo with a fruity aroma.

Pleased with her purchases, Eden decided to call into the Centre on her way home from town.

She had a couple of hours before she needed to prepare for work at the library that afternoon.

Christine and Mike Brewer were there, as were Edith Hunt and several others. They were painting the inside of the largest room in which most activities were held, including Church on a Sunday morning.

Eden was welcomed warmly and was handed a paint brush. She laughed, and joined in the labour, telling those present that the paint job was looking good. This was good medicine for the young lady as the conversation was splashed with humour – just what she needed at this time. Eden had told no-one, apart from Dorothy Moore and Vicky Morgan, about her fertility problems. Both had been sympathetic and each had promised to pray for the couple, for which both Eden and Mark were grateful.

As she began to paint alongside her friends at the Centre, Eden joined in with their lighthearted banter. Edith Hunt, who was an older woman, told the group that she had endeavoured to lure her husband away from his favourite television programme in order to help with the painting. She laughed, telling them that it had been an impossible task to pull him away from his all important quiz show. She had then compromised by telling her hubby that she expected a hearty dinner to be cooked and ready to eat when she returned home that evening. However, she didn't believe for a moment that he would actually cook dinner. "He'll probably be asleep in his arm chair when I get home," she told the small group, who laughed and began to tell their humorous 'husband' stories.

"Mark, of course, is the perfect husband." Eden gave a giggle before admitting that she had become so frustrated at her husband's seeming inability to remember to put his socks and his underwear into the laundry basket to have them washed, that she threatened to leave them unwashed if he didn't begin doing it.

"So, what happened?" Christine Brewer asked.

Eden replied that Mark had begun to put his laundry in the basket, but that it had been a short term thing. "It's easier to do it myself," she stated.

The other women grinned, and Edith, with an exaggerated sigh, said, "Men!" adding that they couldn't do without them though. The group laughed and agreed.

Eden left the Centre having been encouraged and feeling relaxed.

She arrived home and, after a quick lunch, headed off to the library to begin work. She was quite glad that, as it was Friday, she would have the next two days off, and planned to do something special with her husband, as they hadn't spent much quality time together lately.

She had been experiencing a mild nausea as well as being aware of a continuous dull headache.

She realized these were probably side effects of the medication she was ingesting. However, these symptoms were very mild and she was easily able to cope with them. Besides, she had taken the final pill in the five day course that morning, and was filled with a mix of anticipation and anxiety, knowing that all that she and Mark could do now was wait – and, of course, pray for the treatment to have been successful.

Time alone would tell.

CHAPTER SIX

Finally, the day of Mark's birthday arrived and down at the Centre, it was all hands to the deck. Decorations were being put up and tables prepared for food and for the placing of birthday gifts.

Before Mark left for work that morning, Eden had made him a special breakfast, and had also given him a small gift, promising him that they would do something special to celebrate the day when he returned from work.

"By the way," she had said to him as he was leaving for work, "would you mind calling into the Centre to pick me up on your way home from work? I have some things that I need to work on there."

"Of course, honey," an unsuspecting Mark had replied.

After kissing his bride gently on the forehead, he had walked out the door.

Eden had taken the afternoon off work at the library that day in order to have plenty of time to prepare for the festivities of the evening's surprise party. There was a group of people there to assist her.

She left the Centre to go and pick up the all important

birthday cake. The cake shop had done a fabulous job of making and decorating it and Eden was thrilled. She laid it in the middle of one of the tables when she returned, covering it with a light table cloth amongst ooh's and ahh's from those who were present to help.

"It's beautiful!" Christine Brewer remarked. "I'm sure that Mark will love it."

Others agreed and all were impressed with the rectangular shaped, two layered cake which was covered with blue icing and sported a racing car made entirely of chocolate on the top layer.

The words, 'Happy birthday, Mark,' had been spelled out in white icing, and Eden looked forward to unveiling it for him that evening.

At about 4pm, those who had been invited to the birthday tea began to arrive, carrying meals that they had concocted, to share, as well as gifts for Mark. All of these were placed on the tables which, by this time, had been formed into a long line along the length of the room. Dorothy Moore, as well as some of the other women, was busy in the kitchen area, buttering scones and icing lamingtons which had been made by Viki Morgan. Viki had also taken the day off work to help her cousin with preparations for the party.

As 5pm approached, the Centre had certainly been transformed by the hard work of Eden and her friends. The tables were full of tasty looking home made meals including quiches, casseroles, and a variety of other types of dishes which had been created for the pot luck dinner by those attending.

By 5.30pm everyone had arrived at the Centre and all

were waiting with anticipation for the 'Birthday Boy' to turn up. There would have been about forty people in all waiting there for the guest of honour to arrive. At about 6.20pm Eden looked at her watch, telling those gathered that Mark must have been held up at work. She walked outside to the front of the building to wait for him, with growing excitement.

However, she was a little frustrated as Mark was late. The food had been heated up and everyone was gathered waiting for him. He should have well and truly arrived by this time, so Eden walked back inside to phone Mark's work to see what was holding him up. After looking in the phone book for the number, she was about to dial out when the phone rang. Picking up the receiver she answered. To her surprise, the caller was Mark himself.

"Where are you?" she asked him, beginning to feel a little anxious.

"Honey," Mark replied. "I'm sorry, but I cannot collect you from the Centre tonight."

He continued to speak, telling Eden not to be alarmed but that he had been involved in a minor car accident and was at the local medical unit.

"What? Are you okay?" Eden began to panic.

Mark reassured her, telling her that he was fine, but had been admitted overnight to the Medical Centre purely for observation as he had lost consciousness for a couple of minutes in the crash. He insisted that he felt fine and that both he and the occupants of the other car had escaped injury.

"They just want me to stay here overnight as a precaution," he told Eden, who asked how the accident had happened.

Mark replied that a car had driven through a stop sign in town and had hit his vehicle side on.

"I am sorry, sweetheart," he said. "I know that you were planning to have a special time with me for my birthday but can we plan something for tomorrow night?" he asked.

"I told the doctor that I was fine but they wanted to keep me in just for the night." He added that their car had not been as fortunate as he had and had been quite badly damaged. Eden drew a long breath, grateful that Mark seemed to be uninjured, and told him that she would visit him at the unit shortly. She said nothing to Mark of the party that had been planned for him. She hung up the phone with a mix of concern for the man she loved, and disappointment that the hard work of preparing his surprise party had been a wasted exercise.

She told the people at the Centre what had happened and apologized for the fact that all of their hard work had been for nothing.

Dorothy spoke up stating that the party could well be held the following evening when Mark was released from the Medical Centre. "Some of this food can be safely stored overnight," she said.

"Why can't we postpone Mark's party for twenty four hours?" she asked. Everyone agreed including Eden, who apologized for having to leave to be with Mark. She felt bad leaving the work to others.

However, all were in high spirits and readily agreed to pitch in and do whatever was necessary to put the party off until the following evening. All were pleased that Mark had no injury other than a bit of a bump on the head. They told

Eden to visit with her husband while they organized things at the Centre. A grateful Eden, after asking them to pray, hurried off to visit Mark at the medical unit.

When she arrived, she found Mark sitting in the small lounge watching television. The couple embraced and Mark made them both coffee.

The sole nurse on duty that night was busy in another room, so Mark and Eden enjoyed some privacy. Eden was relieved to see Mark in good spirits and looking well. She spent a couple of hours with him before he urged her to return home to get some sleep.

"You will be able to pick me up in the morning, sweetheart," Mark told his wife.

Eden replied that it would be lonely at home without him but she was glad that he hadn't been seriously injured.

"I am just here for the night for observation," Mark said and Eden suggested that he get some rest.

After walking back with him to his white clinical looking hospital bed, she kissed him and promised to come down to collect him first thing in the morning.

Mark stated that they would have to sort out what to do with his car which had needed to be towed away.

"Never mind thinking about that now," Eden replied before leaving her husband to return home for the night.

When Eden finally went to bed that evening, she tossed and turned, somehow unable to wind down for sleep. It had been a big day and she missed sleeping with Mark at her side.

"Never mind," she consoled herself. "He will be home again in the morning," and holding to that comforting thought, she eventually drifted off into a peaceful and lengthy sleep. Little did she know that disaster was just around the corner.

In fact she slept for longer than she had intended and was woken abruptly by the sound of the telephone ringing the next morning.

"Hello!" she greeted the caller. It was a nurse from the Medical Centre, and Eden was expecting to be asked to come down and take Mark home. However, the nurse made no mention of taking Mark home and requested that Eden come immediately down to the unit.

When Eden asked if anything was wrong, the nurse was evasive but repeated that Eden needed to come to the unit as soon as possible.

With rising concern, she dressed quickly and jumped into her car heading to the medical unit where she was met by a nurse at the clinic's entrance. Eden noticed that an ambulance was parked at the front of the building. The nurse ushered her past Mark's room, where the door was closed, and into an office where one of the doctors was waiting to speak with her.

Eden was gasping for breath, with her anxiety at an incredibly high level, as she asked the doctor with a trembling voice what was wrong with Mark, and why was the door to his room closed?

CHAPTER SEVEN

After motioning Eden to sit down, the doctor cleared his throat and began to speak to her.

"It seems that there has been some kind of complication regarding your husband's health," he said.

Eden sat rigidly in the chair as the doctor continued to speak.

"Mark awoke this morning complaining that he was unable to move his legs," he told Eden. "It seems also that he is unable to walk."

Eden began to sob as she choked out a barrage of questions to the doctor who patiently endeavoured to answer them.

"We know very little at this stage," he stated. "However, this seeming paralysis is unlikely to be connected with the motor vehicle crash that your husband was involved in yesterday, although I guess it's possible," he said with a shrug. "We have no answers as to how this could have happened."

He continued to speak, telling Eden that Mark was being prepared to be transferred by ambulance to a hospital in the city where he would be admitted and thoroughly examined by one of the specialists there in an effort to determine what had caused the problems. Eden began to tremble again with fear and distress and asked if she could see her husband.

"Certainly," the doctor replied, and a nurse, who had been sitting in on the conversation, escorted Eden to Mark's room.

As one would expect, Mark was distressed, too, and the couple clung to one another. The nurse informed Eden that he had been given a mild tranquilizer in preparation for the trip to West End City Hospital, which was to happen shortly. She then left them alone, closing the door as she exited the room.

"I'm frightened," Mark spoke to his wife in a low voice.

Although Eden was engulfed in fear herself, she did her best to hide it as she softly spoke to the man she loved.

"We will get through this together, sweetheart."

She gently ruffled his short mousey hair and did her best to reassure her husband while worrying herself about what would happen now.

There was a knock at the door and a nurse entered the room, followed by two ambulance personnel who rolled in a stretcher.

"It's time to go to West End City Hospital now," the nurse said, adding that she was sure that they would take great care of Mark. Eden bent over Mark and told him that she would travel to the hospital in her own vehicle.

Mark was shuffled carefully onto the stretcher and wheeled to the waiting ambulance where it was hoisted inside. The back of the ambulance was closed and the journey to the city began.

After jumping into her car, Eden drove home where she quickly packed some toiletries as well as pyjamas for Mark, then set off for the hospital, praying for the entire length of the trip.

Mark was taken to the Emergency Department of the City Hospital, from where he was to be assigned to a ward.

Upon her arrival, Eden parked her vehicle and went inside to wait with Mark for the attending surgeon to examine and admit him.

An hour or so later, Mark was wheeled into a single room in Ward 4a which was one of the hospital's surgical wards, with Eden accompanying him. The smallish room was painted a cream colour and contained a cabinet which was next to the bed. Mark was rolled from the ambulance trolley onto a clinical looking hospital bed with crisp white linen. Eden proceeded to empty the contents of the small suitcase she had packed for her husband and to put the contents into the cabinet.

"I have some pyjamas for you, hun," she told Mark who didn't respond.

Eden told him that it would be best for the nurses to help him into his nightwear as she didn't want to do anything to inadvertently injure him.

Left alone for a while in the room, Eden pulled up a chair next to the bed in which her husband lay.

The couple were silent as Eden clung to Mark's hand. It was extremely difficult for her to have to watch her normally strong and independent husband in a position such as this.

"Would you like me to see if I can get you a hot drink, sweetheart?" she eventually asked.

Mark shrugged his shoulders and asked Eden if she had eaten that day.

"No," she answered. She told him she was not hungry, to which he replied that he didn't think he could eat anything either.

Mark suddenly spoke with tears in his eyes as he looked at Eden and said, "What if I'm never able to walk again?"

Eden soothed him gently and replied that they would work through this situation as a couple whatever the outcome, telling him not to imagine the worst.

"You are here in the hospital so that they can find out what is wrong and hopefully fix it," she said, holding Mark close and rubbing his back as one would soothe a small child.

Eden sat with Mark until lunch for the patients was served. After encouraging Mark to try to eat something, she left the hospital in order to visit Dorothy and to let Mark's close friends know what had happened. She told her husband that she would return to visit him a little later in the day.

Dorothy was horrified at the news about Mark's apparent paralysis. She held Eden close as they both wept.

"I've been trying to be strong for Mark," Eden told her friend, "but inside, I'm falling apart, too, and need someone to be strong for me. I guess I've become used to Mark being the strong one and the person whom I can lean on," she told Dorothy, who responded by quickly assuring Eden that she would support her and do whatever she could to help both Eden as well as Mark.

"Let me make you some lunch," Dorothy stated, and told Eden to sit down as she scurried around the kitchen, making them both a couple of sandwiches and a hot drink.

Eden suddenly realized that she was hungry and was grateful for the food that Dorothy had provided and for the steaming cup of coffee which had also been prepared by the older woman.

"Mark is quite depressed and is frightened that he'll never walk again," Eden said and added, "We both are."

"Sweetheart," Dorothy responded. "God has His hand on both of you and I know that somehow, whatever happens, He will give you both strength, and enable you to get through whatever lies ahead."

She squeezed Eden's hand, and suggested that they arrange a roster of the couple's friends to assist with visiting Mark.

"You will only wear yourself out if you are ever up at the hospital. I know that you are worried but you need to allow your friends to support and help out with whatever they can," she stated.

Eden nodded in agreement.

Dorothy spoke again. "Let me get in touch with Mike and Christine Brewer as well as Vicky and some of Mark's other friends and you can perhaps get in contact with his family."

"Yes," Eden replied. "I've attempted to contact Mark's parents but have been unable to do so. I think that they are away on holiday but I will continue trying to get hold of them," she replied.

Eden had taken time off from her work at the library, filling Jennifer in on what had happened and telling her that she had no idea as to when, or if, she would be able to return to her job there.

Soon after Eden returned to the hospital, Mark's surgeon entered the room, flanked by an entourage of junior doctors including the surgical registrar. He was a tall slim man with thinning grey hair who introduced himself as Mr Weblin. He looked to be in his late fifties and wore a white coat as did those who accompanied him. He smiled at Mark and Eden, then requested that Eden leave the room while he examined his patient.

Eden decided to locate the hospital cafe to sip a coffee while she waited for the doctors to finish with Mark.

"Just maybe," she thought, "they might have some idea of what is wrong, after looking Mark over."

She was realistic in believing that a cursory examination wouldn't produce the answers they were seeking. She realized that Mark would be likely to face a barrage of tests in the doctor's attempts to determine what was wrong with his legs.

When Eden returned to the ward, Mark was once more alone in his room. She asked how the examination had gone and Mark replied that the doctor had done very little.

"He just asked me to try to move my legs."

"And?" Eden asked.

Mark replied that he had been unable to do so. He told Eden that the surgeon had also pricked his legs in various places with some type of sharp instrument and also scraped the soles of his feet asking if he was able to feel it.

"I felt it all," he said, and Eden grew a little more positive in mood to hear this.

Mark spoke again. "Tomorrow they are giving me a full body scan as well as some x-rays and other tests," he explained. "Also, the nurse came in a little earlier and took my blood pressure as well as some blood from me for testing."

Eden looked at his empty lunch tray and remarked that she was glad that he had eaten. Mark gave her a subdued smile as he told her that her cooking was far more palatable than the hospital food.

That evening, Eden was finally able to contact Mark's parents and explain to them what had happened to their son. Alarmed at the news, they promised to drive to the Downes the following day, accepting Eden's offer to have them stay in her and Mark's villa.

Over the next few days, Mark underwent a thorough array of tests in order for the doctors to try to reach a diagnosis for his unusual condition.

Eden visited him at least once daily, along with his parents once they had arrived in town. The couple's friends visited him regularly. These included Dorothy Moore, Vicky Morgan. and many of Mark's work mates. Mike and Christine Brewer were regularly at his bedside also.

Everyone did their best to encourage him. All assured Mark that they were praying for his recovery and for God to give the doctors wisdom for diagnosis and treatment for the young man.

Mark was encouraged to receive so many visitors.

However, he tired easily and needed an increase of time in which to rest.

CHAPTER EIGHT

The staff involved in Mark's care were in a meeting to discuss his test results as well as to make decisions concerning further options for him. Mr Weblin addressed his team.

"Every test to date has come back clear," he stated. "Also, Mark is responsive to painful stimuli. Mark's brain scan, as well as a scan of his entire body, has given no clues as to what could be wrong. We have also tested him for several medical conditions without finding anything. I am at a loss to know what is causing this man's problems," he stated. "In fact," he continued, "I am wondering if Mark's condition could possibly be psychosomatic in nature and brought on as a result of mental trauma in response to his accident. I have come up empty handed concerning anything physical that might have caused his problems. As a medical team, rather like putting together a jigsaw puzzle, we collect the information provided by testing, in order to make an accurate diagnosis for each patient that we see. In the case of Mark Hansen, I simply cannot join the dots."

He continued to speak. "In order to make certain that I have not missed anything, I will ask another surgeon to review the test results and to examine this patient to provide a second opinion. However, I am certain that I have carried out every relevant test, and that after extensive testing, there is no evidence to suggest that Mark has a physical problem which is keeping him from being able to move his legs or to walk. I will speak with Mr Wilkinson and ask him to take a look at Mr Hansen before calling for a psychiatric consultation. This case is quite an unusual one. I will speak with the patient later in the day," he added.

With those words, the meeting was over and the medical team disbanded.

When Eden arrived at the hospital a short time later, two male nurses were pushing a wheelchair into Mark's room. She and Mark looked at them. One explained that Mr Weblin wanted Mark to begin to get used to being mobile.

"Have they found out what's wrong with me?" Mark asked anxiously. "Am I going to be bound to this chair for life?" he enquired.

The nurses replied that the surgeon would come to have a talk with Mark shortly and that they were unable to answer his questions before he had seen the specialist.

Together they moved Mark over to the edge of the bed and eased him into the wheelchair, lifting his legs to place his feet on the foot rests.

"Don't leave the room until the doctor has been to see you," one of the nurses told him as they exited Mark's hospital room.

Eden and Mark sat quietly, waiting for Mr Weblin to visit them.

"I wonder what he'll have to say," Mark said and Eden nodded her head, wondering the same thing.

They didn't have long to wait, as within ten minutes the surgeon arrived. He was alone and, with a smile, he pulled up a chair and spoke to Mark.

"You have undergone thorough testing in order for us to try to pin point what might be causing your problems," he said. "All of these tests have been clear and I have been unable to find a reason for your disability – at least a physical one."

Eden stared at the doctor and asked him what he was saying.

The surgeon replied that it was quite probable that Mark's condition stemmed from a psychological problem – possibly due to the trauma of his car accident."

Eden looked incredulously at the doctor before asking him if he believed that Mark was fabricating his inability to walk.

"Not at all," Mr Weblin replied. "This is very real for Mark and the mind can be very powerful. If his brain is giving him the message that he is unable to walk, then his condition is as real as a physical one would be. The difference is that it is rooted in his mind instead of in his body. This condition is called a psychosomatic disorder and will need to be treated by a specialist in the area of mental health."

Both Eden and Mark gasped, as they had been unprepared for the possibility that Mark was suffering from a mental health problem.

The doctor told them that, in order to make certain that he hadn't missed anything, he was going to provide a second opinion for Mark.

"I will ask a colleague to examine you and to review your test results before asking for a psychiatric consultation for you," he advised Mark. "Do you have any questions?" he asked the couple.

Eden immediately spoke, asking the doctor if Mark was in this condition purely because his mind was telling him that it was real.

"In a nutshell, yes," Mr Weblin replied. "However, it is a bit more complicated than that."

He continued to speak explaining to Eden that the mind held great power, even over the body, and that because Mark's mind was telling him that he couldn't walk, it was actually manifesting in his body.

"We believe that this disorder was almost certainly brought on by the mental trauma of the car crash that your husband has been involved in."

"How is it fixed?" Eden asked.

Mr Weblin paused before replying. "Mark will need intensive psychological treatment. However, this won't guarantee that his condition will be reversed," he said.

Eden was distressed and asked the specialist why Mark couldn't just tell himself that he was not paralyzed and be returned to normal.

The doctor explained that the mind is a very complicated part of the body.

"It would be great if these things were fixed that easily," he replied. "But, unfortunately, they are not easily righted. You both need to know that there is a possibility that Mark will not recover."

At this, Mark, who had been growing increasingly angry throughout the conversation, spoke to the doctor, telling him that his condition was indeed a physical problem and inferred that the surgeon had not tested him thoroughly enough to diagnose the problem.

"There's nothing wrong with my mind," he insisted in a loud voice.

Mr Weblin spoke gently to the angry and frustrated Mark, telling him that he would, as he had promised to do, get another opinion for him.

"However," he added, "if Mr Wilkinson cannot find a physical cause for your illness, we are going to have to do our best to help you in other ways."

He then stood up and looked somewhat apologetically at the couple, telling them that he would leave them for now in order for them to attempt to digest some of the information he had given them. As he left the room, he told Mark that his colleague would call in to examine him in the next day or so, advising him to use the wheelchair as much as possible in order to get used to it.

When the doctor had left, Mark, who was furious about what he had been told, refused to engage in further conversation with Eden. She embraced her husband and left the hospital, in order to give him some time to calm down, and herself some much needed time to process what the doctor had told them.

She had an appointment to attend the following morning, and was distracted and deep in thought.

Eden was glad that Mark's parents spent most of that day

visiting with their son as she wanted to be alone. The young lady had much on her mind, including the information given them by the surgeon.

Dropping to her knees, she prayed fervently for half an hour or more, asking the God Whom she loved and served, to make a way for her and for Mark.

The following afternoon, when Eden arrived at the hospital, Mark's fury had heightened. He was raving about the nurses who had told him that he had walked in his sleep overnight.

"It's not true," he insisted. "They are making this up because they cannot find out what is wrong with me and are putting me into the too hard basket," he fumed.

Eden was sitting quietly and really wasn't taking in much of what her husband was saying. He continued to vent his anger stating that the hospital staff were not doing their job and that the doctor's had failed him.

"What?" Eden replied.

It was obvious that she had something on her mind and Mark, still angry, asked her what was wrong.

Eden paused before bursting into tears, and in the midst of intense sobbing, blurted out to Mark that she was pregnant. Mark stared at her open mouthed, and his distressed wife ran from the room.

CHAPTER NINE

Eden jumped into her car heading out of the hospital and towards the Downes. She continually brushed aside the tears which threatened to obscure her vision. Finally, she pulled up in front of Dorothy Moore's house and knocked on the door, once more becoming overwhelmed with the tears that flooded her eyes and rolled down her cheeks. Dorothy opened the door, and seeing that Eden was distressed, immediately ushered her inside and into her lounge where she sat with her younger friend on the couch embracing her and rubbing her slim shoulders. Eden tried to stifle her tears.

Eventually, she was able to speak. "I walked out on Mark," she told Dorothy who placed an arm around Eden's shoulders and invited her to talk some more. "Oh, Dorothy!" Eden said, beginning to sob again. "I'm pregnant and Mark is stuck in a wheelchair without any physical reason for it, and maybe for life," she told the older woman.

Taken by surprise, Dorothy stared at Eden for a moment then held her close and soothed her young friend as best she could.

Eden continued to choke out her words. "I don't know

what to do," she wept. "All of our dreams have shattered," she told Dorothy, who sat in silence listening to Eden, and uselessly endeavouring to comfort her.

Eventually, Dorothy spoke, telling Eden that she would be happier if the younger woman would stay overnight with her. "It would be better for you to sleep here tonight rather than stay alone now that Mark's parents have returned home," she stated. "I will make up the bed in the guest room for you. How does that sound?" she asked Eden, adding that she didn't feel comfortable with the idea of her staying alone in the state that she was in. Eden accepted the older lady's offer with gratitude.

Dorothy then went to the kitchen to make a snack for Eden who had confessed to not having eaten all day. She also made a mug of hot chocolate for them both.

The telephone rang and Dorothy picked it up in the kitchen. She spoke with the caller in a low voice for a few minutes then, replacing the receiver, continued with what she had been doing.

Entering the lounge once more with a sandwich and a hot drink for Eden, she informed her friend that the caller had been Mark who was concerned for Eden and had guessed that she was here after having been unable to reach her at home.

"I can't cope with talking to him right now," Eden replied, and Dorothy said that she understood and had told Mark that Eden needed a day or so as she was overwhelmed and exhausted.

"Maybe you will be able to talk with him after a good night's sleep," she told her young friend who nodded in agreement.

"I just need a little space," she told Dorothy who was quick to agree.

"You are both carrying a heavy load," she remarked.

Although Eden was unable to manage to eat the sandwich, she sipped quietly on the cup of hot chocolate that Dorothy had made for her.

The two women retired early to bed that evening and both slept soundly.

Eden awoke the following morning feeling refreshed and considerably more positive in mood. She joined Dorothy who was in the kitchen preparing breakfast and remarked that whatever Dorothy was cooking smelled great.

"Good!" Dorothy replied. "We are having a good full breakfast. How do hash browns and eggs sound?" she asked Eden, who responded with a smile, telling her friend that the breakfast sounded wonderful.

"All homemade, of course," Dorothy added, and invited Eden to be seated at the dining table as the food was almost ready. They both ate a hearty breakfast, and then stayed sitting at the table sipping cups of tea.

Dorothy spoke to Eden, gently asking her when she found out she was pregnant.

Eden replied, "I thought I might be, but it was confirmed at a doctor's appointment only yesterday," she replied. Her voice trembled as she spoke again to Dorothy telling her that this was so far from the dream that she and Mark had cherished for such a long while.

"Things couldn't be worse," she continued as the tears spilled down her face. "Nothing has worked out in the way that we hoped it would," she sobbed.

Dorothy touched her friend lightly on the shoulder before

agreeing that so many times our dreams don't turn out in the way that we expect them to and hope that they will.

"I must go to visit Mark," Eden stated, wiping the tears from her eyes. "He and I need to talk," she told Dorothy who nodded in agreement.

"The nursing staff said that he walked in his sleep a couple of nights ago," Eden said. "If he can walk while he's asleep, why can he not walk while awake? I just don't understand," she sighed.

Dorothy replied that some of the emotional trauma that people experience can have a great impact upon them physically. "Although I am far from an expert," she admitted.

When Eden arrived at the hospital later in the day, Mark was once again sitting in his wheelchair.

As soon as he saw his bride, tears filled his eyes as he asked her forgiveness for the way that he had taken his anger out on her the previous day. Eden, in turn, apologised for leaving him so abruptly and she bent over to embrace her husband who held her close and kissed her.

"I have been examined by a second surgeon this morning and he is going over my test results," he reported, stating also that he was hoping that this new doctor would discover what was wrong with him.

"I was stunned to hear that you are pregnant, my beautiful wife," Mark said, then added, "This is all the more reason that they need to find and fix what is wrong with me. I don't want to be a new father who is stuck in a wheelchair."

Eden, although a little subdued, managed to smile. "Yes,"

she replied. "We are finally going to be parents. God has indeed done a miracle."

Mark responded by promising to look after Eden and their baby. "I just need to get well and out of this chair," he stated.

Eden made no reply to his words, instead straightening the covers on Mark's bed in an attempt to conceal the tears which were threatening to overwhelm her again. Composing herself, she turned to face him and told him that he would be a great father to their child. "You have a loving and gentle personality. Our child will be very fortunate to have you as his or her dad," she stated with a conviction that she genuinely felt. Mark responded by reminding Eden of how much he loved her.

"And I love you, too," she replied.

The couple clung to one another as the tears of both fell unabated. In that moment, both of them experienced a special kind of closeness – one which had been, in part, dulled since the time of Mark's accident.

Eden spoke softly to her husband. "We will get through this together," she whispered, "and regardless of what happens, we have been joined by God. You are my husband and I love you dearly."

Mark responded by affirming his love for Eden also. He thanked her for the patience that she had been showing him and reassured her that he would soon be able to walk again provided that the doctors did their job properly.

Eden remained silent, then suggested that she push Mark in his wheelchair down to the hospital cafeteria so they could have a cup of coffee. "You need to get out of this room for a break," she added.

Mark agreed, but said that he would wheel himself. They headed to the hospital cafe where they enjoyed a hot drink as well as a snack. Eden was concerned to notice that Mark had lost a considerable amount of weight in just a short time, and she asked him if he had been eating.

"Not well," he admitted, blaming the hospital food which he said was bland and unappetising.

"I will bring you in some home cooked meals," Eden promised, and Mark responded with a smile and a grateful thanks.

Shortly after the couple returned to Mark's room, there was a knock on the door and a tall, thin man with greying hair entered the room. He was dressed in a dark-coloured suit and he introduced himself as Doctor Jeffrey Fanshaw.

"Are you another surgeon?" Mark asked.

Doctor Fanshaw smiled and replied that he was one of the hospital's psychiatrists.

"I have been asked to have a chat with you," he told Mark who immediately turned away from him stating that as there was nothing mentally wrong with him. He did not need the services of a psychiatrist.

Doctor Fanshaw smiled again and endeavoured to reassure Mark, telling him that he merely wanted to talk with him, and that if it was unnecessary, he would not return for another meeting.

"Does that sound okay?" he asked, and Mark reluctantly

replied that he had better come in. He also insisted that Eden remain in the room during the interview.

"That's fine," the doctor said, and pulling up a chair, he sat down and began to ask Mark a series of questions, beginning with what Mark remembered about his car accident. Mark gave him short answers to his questions, making it obvious that he didn't want to speak with this expert in mental health.

"My disability is not a mental one," he told the doctor, who, in reply stated that he believed that Mark's condition was indeed very real.

"We all recognize the seriousness of what has happened to you, as well as the implications of that upon your life." He continued to speak. "There is some confusion, though, as to how you came to be paralyzed, and that is the reason that I have been called in to talk with you. We are all wanting to get to the bottom of how you have become confined to a wheelchair and we do not want to leave any stone unturned. Tell me, Mark," Doctor Fanshaw asked. "Have you ever walked in your sleep?"

Mark's reply was an instant and sullen, "No!"

Eden glared at her husband who continued to speak to the doctor telling him that the nursing staff had accused him of sleep walking several nights ago but that they had fabricated this information.

"That's fine, Mark," the psychiatrist replied. "I am not here to upset you."

Mark's voice rose as he became angry. "You don't believe me, do you?" he asked the doctor accusingly.

Doctor Fanshaw responded by telling Mark that he would leave him to get some rest, and maybe they could meet again shortly. The psychiatrist realised that Mark was becoming upset and decided that to question him further at that time would not be beneficial to him. He smiled at Eden and Mark, thanking them for their time as he left the room.

CHAPTER TEN

Mr Weblin, the specialist who had been the first to examine Mark, stood just outside the closed door to his patient's room. He had read the notes which had been written by his colleague, Mr Wilkinson. They were in agreement with his own review of his patient's condition, as was also the initial report from the psychiatrist, which stated that his patient was in denial and unwilling to consider that his condition was in any way related to any type of mental disorder.

Taking a deep breath, he entered Mark's room, flanked by his team of junior doctors and a surgical registrar.

"How are you this morning?" he asked Mark who replied that he would be a great deal better if the doctor had managed to discover the cause of his condition, and begin treatment for it.

Mr Weblin began to speak to Mark telling him that he, as well as the two of his colleagues who had examined him, were certain that his condition was due to a psychosomatic disorder. They had all agreed that his problem was not physical in origin.

Mark did not respond. He was discouraged, as well as frustated, to be consistently told that his inability to walk was caused in some way by a malfunction in his mind. He was unable to understand this way of thinking and was sure that the doctors had reached an erroneous conclusion.

Mr Weblin continued to speak to his patient. "We are going to transfer you to spend some time back in your local medical unit in Shackellby Downes," he told Mark, who quickly looked at him, asking the doctor if he was really going to discharge him from hospital without having treated his problem.

The specialist told Mark that he was going to arrange for the young man to be supported by a full time attendant carer at home. He also stated that Mark would remain in the Downes' medical unit while his villa was modified in order for him to be able to live in his wheelchair at home. He added that the hospital would foot the bill for the renovations that would be necessary for Mark to return home.

"I also strongly advise that you attend regular sessions with a trained psychologist, meeting with him regularly here at the hospital. This holds the best chance of your regaining your ability to walk," he stated. "Your vehicle will also need to be modified in order for your wheelchair to be loaded in and out of it," he told Mark who stared at the ground without speaking. His vehicle had been too badly damaged in the accident to be of any use.

"Do you have any questions?" the surgeon asked.

Mark replied that, while he had no questions, he was adamant that he would not see a psychologist and that he fully believed that his disability was due to some type of physical problem. He stated, also, that he believed that the doctors had not done their job by neglecting to give a reasonable explanation as to why he was paralyzed.

Mr Weblin spoke with sympathy to the young man, telling him that he wished the best for him. He informed him that his transfer back to Shackellby Downes would take place that afternoon and that he would be meeting the man who was to care for his needs before he was discharged. Mr Weblin then exited the room, flanked by his entourage of junior doctors. He closed the door to Mark's room behind him, and Mark, sitting in his wheelchair, placed his head in his hands weeping with disappointment.

The fact that the doctors seemed to be unable to help him, was beginning to sink in and he was distressed at having to face life confined to a wheelchair. He thought about Eden and about the baby that they were expecting, and wondered how things could be any worse for him and for his family. There would certainly need to be some major adapting needed in his life, as well as in the lives of his family and friends.

Meanwhile, Eden, who was preparing to leave home to head to the hospital to visit Mark, was surprised to receive a phone call from him, during which he explained to her all that the doctor had told him.

"It's probably better for you to wait until I am home in the Downes this afternoon rather than driving all this way to visit me when I'm returning home," he stated.

Eden was surprised to hear of Mark's impending discharge from hospital. She agreed to wait until he had settled into the local Medical Centre before visiting, and wondered again, as she had often done lately, how the couple would manage with Mark confined to a wheelchair. It was a relief to know that her husband would be given an attendant carer who would assist in a practical way with Mark's needs, as Eden realized that she would struggle greatly had she been given the task of completely looking after her husband – especially now that she had become pregnant. She hoped that the chosen caregiver would be a person who Mark and she were happy with, since he would be spending much time in their home.

Following the recent events, Eden had become tired and discouraged as she contemplated the future, realizing that it was possible that Mark would be wheelchair bound for the rest of his life.

While her heart ached for the man she loved, she also secretly worried about how the couple would cope, especially with a new baby on the way.

Meanwhile, at the hospital, a social worker was visiting Mark with the man who would be his caregiver. She introduced herself as Keri Drake and the man who accompanied her as Fredrick Willans.

Fred stretched out his arm and he and Mark shook hands. Mark replied to his cheery, "Good morning!" with a subdued greeting. Fredrick told his new client to call him Fred, and Mark smiled in reply. Fred was a tall, solidly built man who appeared to be in his late thirties or early forties. His short hair was dark in colour and his eyes sparkled with enthusiasm. He spoke to Mark in an attempt to lighten the atmosphere, telling him that he was sorry that Mark had become wheelchair dependent, but assuring him that he was a great driver, as well as one with lots of experience.

Mark smiled slightly again in response to Fred's comments and asked his new caregiver what his hours of work would be and also what his specific tasks were. Fred smiled and replied that he would be with Mark and Eden to assist with Mark's care from 8am to 8pm daily and that his work would entail a variety of activities, including showering Mark and attending to his hygiene in general. Also, he would accompany Mark and Eden when they went out – at least until Mark became more competent in using his wheelchair. He was also there to attend to any necessary lifting that Mark needed and to generally help out in whatever way was needed.

"The aim is for you to become, over time, as independent as possible," Fred told Mark.

He seemed to be a friendly person. Mark began to warm to him in spite of himself as they chatted.

His good sense of humour gradually put Mark at ease as the visit progressed.

"Have you done this type of work for long?" Mark enquired.

Fred responded immediately that he had worked as a carer for the last ten years having been employed as an electrician before that. Mark perked up a little then and looked at him with a wry grin, telling Fred that he was a trained electrician himself. Fred smiled and suggested lightheartedly that, between the two of them, Mark and Eden's home would certainly be kept from any long term electrical problems.

Mark grinned and agreed.

Ms Drake told Mark that Fred lived in the city and would travel to Shackellby Downes each week day to assist him. Mark was to have a separate carer on the weekends. This man would be introduced to Mark sometime after he had been transferred home.

Ms Drake continued to speak. "We are hoping to gradually reduce your dependence on attendant care," she explained to Mark who nodded to show that he understood.

The social worker then left the two men to further get to know one another. Before exiting the room, she left a card with her details on Mark's bedside cabinet in case he needed to contact her.

After Keri had gone, Fred suggested that he and Mark talk some more over a cup of coffee in the hospital's cafe, and the two left Mark's room with Fred walking beside the wheelchair while Mark pushed himself to the elevator which they entered, travelling to the ground floor where the cafe was situated.

Over coffee, Mark asked his carer why he had decided to work in this area.

Fred replied, "My uncle was eventually confined to a wheelchair after having been diagnosed with multiple sclerosis," he told Mark. Fred then explained that it had been difficult for the family to secure good care for his uncle and that Fred had left his job to look after him in the latter stages of his illness in order to make certain that he was cared for properly. After his uncle's death, Fred had undertaken training to become a carer and had begun to work with others who were wheelchair bound.

"Unfortunately," he stated, "it was difficult to find a compassionate carer and I wanted to do my bit to help to change that for disabled people."

Mark was encouraged by Fred's answer and was hopeful that he had been assigned the best person for the job.

"Are you married?" Mark asked him.

Fred replied that he was divorced and had been put off marriage for now. The two men then left the cafe with Mark wheeling himself back to his room in the ward while Fred walked alongside him.

Fred then left Mark to prepare for his transfer back to the Downes telling him that he would begin work assisting him when he had arrived at his local Medical Unit. He also told Mark that he was looking forward to meeting with Eden and that he believed that he would be able to be an asset to the family.

Mark experienced much relief after having met his new carer whom he believed to be a genuinely caring man. He was also sure that Eden would get on well with Fred.

CHAPTER ELEVEN

With the hospital having officially given the 'go ahead' for work to begin on Eden and Mark's villa, there were several tradesmen at the property, as the bathroom was being revamped in order for Mark to access it in his wheelchair. The bath had been taken out and the shower was being remodelled in order for him to be wheeled into the room to be showered. Also, work had begun on building a ramp at the back of the house. This ramp would lead to the couple's front door which, fortunately, was wide enough for his chair to fit through. Mark had settled into the small medical unit while these alterations were being attended to. Fred had begun caring for Mark there.

Eden was impressed by her husband's carer, as Mark had thought she would be. She was relieved to find him to be a competent and enthusiastic worker who treated Mark with dignity as well as with compassion.

Fred insisted that, as much as was practical, Mark should wheel himself around in order to strengthen his arms and his upper body. Mark spent his time both being in his chair and resting in bed, as he found it quite tiring to move around in his wheelchair. Fred massaged his client's legs and did all that he could to prevent Mark from getting pressure sores. A soft cushion on the seat of his chair assisted with this.

Finally, after two weeks or so, with the modifying of the house complete, Mark moved back home, taken by ambulance. Eden and Mark also realized that they would need to invest in a vehicle which would be able to transport Mark's chair. Because his vehicle had been written off following his accident, with Fred's help, they looked around car yards in the city to find a suitable vehicle.

Eventually, they purchased a four wheel drive vehicle which they both liked the look of and which would also suit their needs. They needed to draw on their savings to add to the money paid out by their car insurance company. The vehicle chosen by the couple was a gray-coloured Toyota Hilux into which Mark's wheelchair fitted perfectly.

Mark's weekend caregiver was very different to Fred and the couple weren't convinced that he was right for the job. However, they decided to give him a try. His name was Troy Foster, and he was of slim build with fair, medium length hair which hung loose around his shoulders. This man was reserved and was an exceptionally quiet person. While this, in itself, wasn't necessarily a bad thing, he showed little enthusiasm for his job and would seat himself in the couple's lounge in order to watch television as often as possible. He did the bare minimum of work, and both Eden and Mark felt uncomfortable around him. After having discussed it, the couple decided to give Troy the benefit of the doubt – and to see if his work to support Mark improved. They agreed to stick with him for a few weeks to see if he would attend to his work with more competence. However, his manner appeared to be off hand and he showed little interest in doing his job. Mark did his best to avoid having much in the way of personal cares done by this man, and both he and Eden were unimpressed with Troy's care of Mark as well as his general attitude. It soon became apparent that Troy was lazy and was not a suitable carer for Mark. The couple decided to contact the hospital's social worker, Keri Drake, to discuss what could be done about this awkward situation.

Meanwhile, they discovered that Fred had been given notice to move out of the apartment which he was renting in the city and was looking for new accommodation. After discussing this, the couple invited Fred to move into their spare bedroom if he wanted to. They offered him free board in exchange for him caring for Mark over the weekends as well. To their delight, Fred accepted their offer and, consequently, Troy was given notice, being told that his services were no longer required. Keri Drake, the social worker, was informed of this change in circumstances, and she said that she saw no problem with the new arrangement if both parties were happy.

Fred settled into Mark and Eden's villa well. The couple were grateful to find that, in addition to caring for Mark, he was willing to help out with cooking as well as with household chores. He gradually became a treasured friend to the couple, who were pleased to have had their problems resolved so easily.

Eden felt completely comfortable with leaving Mark in Fred's care, so she was able to leave the house more often, knowing that her husband was being well looked after. The time for her first check up since becoming pregnant was approaching, and she was feeling a mix of excitement and anxiety as she wondered if all was fine with the baby. She was also becoming frustrated, and even a little angry with Mark, as he was becoming very self-centered as well as self-pitying. He had begun to live with a chip on his shoulder, and to act as though the world owed him something. Eden had endeavoured to be patient and loving towards him. However, her patience was beginning to run thin.

Only a few days ago, while Fred was on a break and away from the house, an appointment card had arrived in the mail for Mark to see one of the hospital's psychologists. After having glanced at it, Mark had flung it to the floor, telling his wife that he had no need of seeing anyone connected to mental health. She had replied sharply, asking Mark who he expected to pick up the card which he had tossed.

"Well, I certainly can't!" he had replied, then had continued his spiel about having received an appointment card of that nature in the first place, as his problem was a physical one and by no means psychological.

Eden, biting her tongue, had walked from the room without replying to her husband.

Fred was also finding Mark increasingly demanding and selfish. However, he showed great patience in caring for the wheelchair bound man who had even begun at times to be rude to him. Fred realized that his patient was frustrated and felt angry at being unable to walk.

However, Eden told him to be firm with Mark who was too often acting like a spoilt child.

"He is taking us for granted," she told him. "It's just not good enough."

Eden expressed her frustrations to Dorothy Moore, telling her that Mark had become almost unbearable to be around at times.

"I just don't understand why he can't walk," she complained to the older woman. "The doctors told us that it was his mind that was telling him that he couldn't move his legs," she told her friend.

"So why is it that his mind cannot also tell him that he can walk again, now that everything has settled down?" Eden asked.

Before Dorothy was able to answer, Eden continued to vent her frustration, going on to say that her husband was refusing to help himself.

"He won't attend any of his appointments with the psychologist," she fumed. "Honestly, Dorothy, it has become as though I am married to a completely different person, and a person who right now I am struggling to even be around," she added, while Dorothy patiently listened.

"This has certainly been a huge change for both Mark and yourself," she told Eden, going on to say that it was not surprising that they were both struggling to cope. She certainly understood the younger woman's frustrations. However, she endeavoured to point out that Mark would be feeling extremely frustrated and angry, too, because of all that had happened to him and the uncertainty concerning whether or not he would ever be able to walk again.

"If it's mind over matter, then it's his choice," Eden retorted, then burst into tears. "I am tired of being his housemaid," she wept, and told Dorothy that Mark showed little gratitude for what was being done for him. "This is no household to bring a new born baby into," she choked out her words.

As Dorothy embraced Eden, she leaned into the older lady's arms, sobbing uncontrollably.

She and Dorothy talked until well into the evening, with Dorothy explaining to Eden that the mind was extremely powerful, and that, while she shouldn't expect too much of herself, she also needed to cut Mark some slack as he was unable to help the fact that he was wheelchair bound.

"He can help his attitude," Eden replied.

"Yes, he can," Dorothy stated, then suggested that Eden imagine how difficult it would be for her if she was in her husband's position.

"You're right, I guess," Eden admitted, and she thanked her friend for being a listening ear.

"I have frustrations, too," she explained, "and I have not been able to express them, because I've been trying to be strong for both Mark and myself. To be honest," she admitted, "the burden is becoming too large for me to cope with."

Dorothy stroked Eden's hair and told her that she understood.

"If you need someone to talk to, I am here," she promised the young lady. She also offered to help with some of the practical things that Eden was attending to, such as the cooking of meals and the performing of household tasks. "You don't need to carry this burden alone," she said.

Eden nodded, grateful for a friend like Dorothy.

They spent the next half hour or so, pre-planning meals which Dorothy had committed to cooking and delivering to the couple for the next week.

"I will also come over twice a week to assist you with the household chores," she promised.

Eden felt considerably better after her time with Dorothy, and returned home in a more positive frame of mind.

CHAPTER TWELVE

Eden attended her medical appointment, having left Mark in the care of Fred. At just over three months into her pregnancy, her stomach had begun to thicken as the new life inside her started to grow. She had needed to buy some larger jeans. However, most of her dresses still fitted her comfortably.

Doctor Mills took her blood pressure and generally checked her over. She pronounced Eden, as well as the unborn baby, to be in good health as far as she was able to tell, and made another appointment for Eden to visit her in two months time. Eden left the surgery in good spirits.

She spoke to the little one inside her, as she often did, telling the unborn baby, whom she and Mark had nicknamed 'peanut,' that he or she would be welcomed and loved.

Instead of returning straight home, she decided to see if her cousin, Vicky Morgan, was free to spend her lunch hour with her as midday was approaching. Eden drove to the bank where Vicky worked as a teller, and spoke to her cousin who replied that she was due for her lunch break shortly and would meet Eden in the mall in about five minutes. They decided to pick up some sandwiches from a cafe to eat in the mall which was a favourite place for the two to meet.

Vicky was the typical tomboy who had stated that she would never want to marry and have children, so Eden was surprised, to say the least, when Vicky sheepishly mentioned that she had met a man.

"No way!" Eden laughed. "Not you!"

"He is a new employee at the bank," Vicky replied, looking somewhat embarrassed. "He is a fun-loving man with a great sense of humour," she told Eden. She asked that Eden keep her secret safe.

Eden howled with laughter, as it had been a standing joke for some years now, that Vicky had never been interested in dating anyone. She had presented herself as an independent young lady who didn't need a man in her life.

When Eden had finished laughing, she solemnly promised not to reveal that her cousin was in love.

"Not in love, silly," Vicky replied, "but we are becoming close friends." She spoke in a low voice as though she was scared that someone would overhear what she was admitting to.

"Can I come to the wedding?" Eden joked.

In reply, Vicky punched her on the shoulder and told her to keep quiet.

"We are just friends, really, at the moment," she stated.

Eden raised her eyebrows and replied that she and Mark had started out as 'just friends'.

Vicky looked at her cousin and reiterated that the friendship between this man and herself probably would never lead to the altar. Eden laughed again and told Vicky that she was good medicine for her.

Vicky replied, "You are mocking me."

Continuing to speak, she said that her views had changed a little bit since meeting Tony whom she claimed was different to most of the men she had met in life thus far.

"Oh, so his name's Tony!" Eden remarked, asking when she could meet him.

"Never!" Vicki retorted. "Or at least, not yet," she replied, with the hint of a smile on her face.

The two young women then giggled as Eden remarked that she had truly not expected her cousin to actually come to 'like' a man. The two chatted for a bit longer, then Vicky needed to return to work.

As she walked away from Eden, she called back over her shoulder, "Remember not a word to anyone."

Eden gave a mock salute and replied that her lips were sealed.

Eden stayed sitting in the mall and smiling to herself. The lunch time interlude with her cousin had done her good, having helped to take her mind off her own problems for a time. Sighing, she finally got to her feet and, walking back to her car, drove home taking the longest route possible. She was not looking forward to interacting with the grumpy and self-centered person Mark had become of late.

That night, as Eden shuffled Mark from the wheelchair, rolling him into bed, she told him that his behaviour had been unacceptable lately.

He responded by telling her that she had never experienced having to live in a wheelchair.

"It's your choice!" she blurted out, then stared at her husband, horrified by what she had just said to him. He looked at her open-mouthed, as tears formed in his eyes and began to trickle down his cheeks.

Eden was quick to apologize, explaining to Mark that she was pregnant and exhausted and that she hadn't meant to speak to him in that way.

"I guess that I have difficulty understanding how you are able to sleep walk, yet cannot seem to use your legs at other times. Also, how you cannot walk, purely because you think that you can't, when there's no physical reason for it," she explained.

Then reaching across the bed, she embraced her husband and he, her. This was something that the couple hadn't done for some time as they had grown apart with the problems which they were facing.

"It's okay, sweetheart," Mark spoke softly. "I need you to believe me, though, when I tell you that my disability is not a figment of my mind – that it stems from some physical cause."

However, Eden was unable to believe her husband, especially as she had actually seen him walk in his sleep several times since his accident.

"That must prove to you that the doctor at the hospital was correct when he told you that your condition was psychological in nature."

Mark became angry, denying once more that he walked in his sleep. He turned away from Eden and endeavoured to sleep.

Eden, facing away from him in their bed, quietly wept until she finally fell into a restless sleep.

As the weeks and then the months passed, it seemed as though Mark and Eden were becoming strangers to one another and they both secretly wondered how long their marriage would last.

Eden was not put off by the fact that Mark was in a wheelchair, but by his angry and cold attitude, especially it seemed, towards her. He had begun to withdraw from her, and in response she had done likewise, unsure of how to navigate her way through life with a man who was so very different to the one whom she had met and married. It was not that she didn't still love Mark.

She did, and sometimes caught glimpses of the man she had known. She was committed to Mark, whatever the implications of that, but they were both miserable much of the time.

Fred was helpful. Eden had been asking him to allow her to help with Mark's care as much as possible. She had learned how to do many of the basic things for her husband, leaving Fred to shower him and change his clothes.

As her pregnancy progressed, she became exhausted more easily and was bearing the consequences of that pretty much on her own, although her friends, including Dorothy, were always offering to help and would often deliver home-cooked meals and turn up to help with household chores.

Eden was grateful for every kindness shown her and Mark. However, the time was definitely drawing closer when she and Mark would need to talk seriously about their marriage and work out a way to restore their relationship, which seemed to be increasingly falling apart around them.

With Eden in her eighth month of pregnancy, the doctors were happy with how everything was progressing. The baby's heartbeat seemed to be strong and all was going well, apart from the fact that her feet had begun to swell. As a result of this, she needed to spend more time with her legs up on a chair, in an effort to bring down the swelling. Also, Eden began to resent Fred's presence in the house so much of the time, as Mark spoke quite freely to his carer while saying very little to her, his wife. However, at other times, she was grateful to have him around, as he was able to assist Mark in ways that she couldn't.

Mark and Eden also argued frequently about money. Although the couple had some savings, Mark had been placed on a disability allowance after his accident as he had become unable to work. This allowance was extremely difficult for him and Eden to survive on, and with a baby on the way, both were concerned about how they would manage financially. Eden, while ideally wanting to be a 'stay at home' mum, was concerned that the low income which the couple were now receiving, would be inadequate to provide for the needs of the family. She worried about this almost ceaselessly, and confided to Dorothy Moore about this looming issue.

Dorothy could see that her young friend was becoming troubled about many things, and she did her best to work out some possible solutions to some of the very real burdens that Eden was carrying.

In fact, Dorothy, although far from wealthy, opened a

savings account into which she regularly placed funds which were assigned especially to assist Eden and Mark raise their baby with a little more financial ease. She invited other friends and family to contribute where they could to this bank account. Many were pleased to join Dorothy in helping Eden and Mark financially, and the savings account slowly but surely grew in funds.

Eden was grateful for all that Dorothy, as well as other friends, was doing, to assist herself and Mark in a variety of ways.

CHAPTER THIRTEEN

Despite Fred's vigilance and his best efforts, Mark had begun to experience the discomfort of a slight pressure sore which was common among those who were wheelchair bound. Eden and Fred accompanied Mark to visit the local doctor who prescribed some cream, as well as advising Mark to spend a little more time out of his chair and resting in bed or on the couch to prevent this problem from becoming more troublesome. Mark was discouraged, as he liked to get out of the house as much as possible in order to socialize with Fred and Eden in his wheelchair. Under Fred's guidance, Eden administered the cream which had been prescribed for Mark, while Fred dressed the area daily, making sure that it was taken care of in the most effective way possible so that it would not become worse. Fortunately, this problem area improved fairly quickly. Mark soon was once more able to gradually increase the periods of time that he spent in his chair on which soft padding was increased to keep him as comfortable as possible.

Meanwhile, Eden and Mark continued to be at loggerheads much of the time and this left them both feeling despondent.

Mark still refused to attend any appointments with a psychologist, insisting that his problem was physical in origin.

Eden decided to see their local doctor, as she had some questions about Mark's disability. She was still unable to understand how a mental condition could affect the body so dramatically. On her visit with Doctor Mills, she asked how it could be that Mark was able to walk in his sleep but seemed at all other times to be unable to use his legs. The doctor replied by explaining to Eden that the mind was a powerful, as well as a complex, part of a person. Also, that when a person experiences trauma, as Mark obviously had done as a result of his car crash, psychosomatic problems could easily be brought on – although she admitted that Mark's disability was a serious and unusual reaction to the emotional trauma which he had sustained.

After having spoken with Doctor Mills, Eden had a slightly clearer picture of how Mark's disability could have come about, yet she struggled with the idea that it was possible for the body to malfunction to such an extent because of a person's mental state, which she was being told was true regarding her husband. She urged Mark to visit with a mental health specialist. However, Mark steadfastly refused to do so. The atmosphere in their home became one of tension as the couple struggled to navigate their daily lives with very little communication between them.

Eden wondered what they could do to sort out their marriage which, by now, was becoming increasingly damaged. She knew that she and Mark needed to communicate honestly with one another. However, this was something which Mark seemed to be actively avoiding engaging in. Eden thought that if they could just go somewhere alone, even for just two or three hours, they might be able to discuss the problems in their marriage without being interrupted.

She knew how to tend to the basic needs that Mark was likely to have over a two or three hour period of time, so she created a plan which she then spoke to Mark about.

A little way into the bush area of the Downes, and a short way up a dirt road, surrounded by bush, there was a little cabin. This cabin was only used now by the odd person starting out on a tramp into the bush clad ranges at the base of the huge mountain, which was part of the incredible scenery in the Downes. The small cabin had been kept in a reasonable standard of repair, and it seemed the perfect place for herself and Mark to retreat to for a short time in order to have a solid and constructive talk about where they were headed as a couple.

Eden told Mark that Fred could drive them up this dirt track in the couple's four wheel drive vehicle, which would easily navigate the track, and be able to collect them again in a few hours.

Eden also explained that she thought that the change of scenery would do the couple good. She could even pack a picnic lunch for them. Mark admitted that their marriage was in trouble and seemed to be receptive to this idea, so they made arrangements with Fred to take them to the cabin on Thursday afternoon. Being three days away, this gave Eden time to prepare a special lunch for Mark and herself. Fred told them that he had business that he needed to do in the city, and that he would attend to this after dropping the couple off and would return to pick them up again when it suited them.

Eden was considerably more positive in mood now that plans were in place for Mark's and her outing and time of uninterrupted talk. She set to work creating a picnic basket in which she included lots of the couple's favourite foods. She found herself singing as she organized this deluxe picnic. It had been a while since she had felt so lighthearted and she was optimistic that she and Mark could engage in some meaningful conversation while away on this little 'date' time in the bush cabin.

Thursday arrived, and Eden, with Fred helping, loaded the picnic box, as well as some other items necessary to care for Mark's needs, into their vehicle. She had filled a thermos flask with hot coffee, and it seemed that all was taken care of. Eden and Mark were excited about this little 'get away' free from the noise of the town. Mark's wheelchair was loaded into the back of the vehicle and they set off in good spirits, with Fred in the driver's seat.

Having arrived at their destination, Eden went in to inspect the cabin. It was in pretty good shape having been maintained by locals.

As a result of heavy rain the evening before, the damp leaves on the track made it a little slippery, so Fred and Eden were extra careful as they unloaded the picnic goodies as well as a folding chair which Fred carried in for Eden to sit on.

At over seven months pregnant, she was now anxiously waiting for the baby's birth. She was uncomfortable with her cumbersome, protruding stomach, and with the swelling in her feet and legs that she was continuing to experience.

The cabin contained a small wooden table and two wooden chairs as well as an antiquated-looking toilet of sorts. Still, it would be enough to suit Eden and Mark's needs for the short amount of time that they would be spending in it.

Fred left the couple, stating that he would return to collect them within three hours time.

Eden placed the basket of goodies onto the wooden table and pulled her chair up close to where Mark's wheelchair was placed. She began to talk to him, telling him that a lot had happened to them both in a short amount of time.

"I feel like you've been slipping away from me," she explained.

Mark nodded in agreement. He then spoke to Eden in a voice which was hoarse with emotion.

"I have been so selfish," he told his wife, "and much of it has been that I feel as though I am a burden to you and cannot believe that you would still love me with the onset of this disability."

He looked at Eden as the tears began to fall from his eyes and roll down his cheeks.

"I've been feeling helpless, as well as of little use to you, as a husband," he sobbed.

Eden had also begun to weep and she extended her hand to Mark who grasped it tightly.

Eden spoke, telling her husband that, although she was unable to understand his condition as well as she would like to, she still loved him deeply, and desperately wanted their marriage to work.

Mark was in complete agreement, and the two engaged in a heart-to-heart talk which was something that they had not done for many months.

As they spoke about their issues, and also about possible ways in which to resolve them, Eden and Mark both dropped their guard and were soon talking earnestly, with all awkwardness overcome.

They spoke honestly and openly about the problems they had been living with, and reaffirmed their love for one another in the midst of their conversation.

After having spoken earnestly for about an hour and a half, the couple, having made an enormous amount of progress, embraced, and just held each other as they sobbed with much relief.

Restoration for this marriage was definitely in progress, and both Eden and Mark knew for certain that many of the barriers which had been keeping them apart had now been dissolved, as they shared with one another their pain and the loneliness which had been experienced by each.

A great deal of healing had been given, as well as received, with both Eden and Mark. Finally, both were certain that their commitment to one another had been established. A break-through had, indeed, happened in their relationship, purely through having really talked over the course of a couple of hours. Both were smiling as Eden leaned over to open the picnic box which was filled with extra special goodies for the couple to feast on.

Suddenly, however, as she bent over the picnic basket, Eden experienced the feeling of some kind of liquid seeping down her legs. She quickly looked down and was horrified to discover that she was bleeding.

"Mark!" she screamed in a panic. "I'm bleeding, and I have no idea why. There is no-one who is able to take me to the hospital."

Mark stared at her in shock as he saw the blood which had begun to steadily flow from between her legs.

Eden tried her best to remain calm. However, she knew, as did Mark, that she needed urgent hospital treatment.

"You have to walk, Mark!" she screamed hysterically. "My life and the life of our baby could be at risk!"

Mark endeavoured to raise himself up in his wheelchair several times but slumped down again, sobbing, and crying out, "I can't walk!"

Eden shrieked at him. "Mark, you need to walk now and you need to get help! The baby and I need help. You simply have to get out of that wheelchair and walk. There's no other way that we can get help!" she screamed.

Then she and her husband broke down, sobbing uncontrollably.

CHAPTER FOURTEEN

Meanwhile, Dorothy Moore, knowing nothing of the situation which was unfolding in the cabin, had just arrived home from town where she had met Christine Brewer for lunch in one of the town's cafes. Kicking off her shoes, she put on her slippers and decided to take a nap in her reclining chair for a while as she was feeling weary having walked to and from town. Her feet were sore and she was looking forward to putting them up.

As she seated herself in her comfortable chair, she glanced at the clock in her lounge which read 1.30pm. She was just beginning to drift into a relaxing sleep when she was abruptly jolted awake by the sound of a voice which seemed to come from somewhere above her. This voice told her to pray for Eden and Mark.

Dorothy knew immediately that she had just heard the audible voice of God, and she trembled as she dropped to her knees and began to pray for the couple, without any idea of why God had commanded her to do so. She prayed earnestly, feeling compelled to pray for safety for Eden and Mark.

Dorothy persisted in fervent prayer. She prayed in the way

that she felt she was being led. She prayed intensely for more than an hour, before she sensed a lifting of the burden which had been placed on her heart for the couple.

At that point, Dorothy knew without being told, that God had answered her prayers even though she was unaware of the reason why she had been called to intercede for the couple.

Climbing awkwardly to her feet, she walked to her telephone and dialed Eden and Mark's number.

There was no answer, so she then rang the Centre to see if they might have popped in there.

Once more, no one answered the phone, so she placed the receiver on the hook and turned her attention to other things while continuing to pray intermittently for Eden and Mark, asking God to provide for her to somehow know if the couple were all right.

She was soon to receive a phone call which would have her standing in absolute awe of God's power, as well as explaining the reason that He had commanded her to pray for Eden and her husband.

Her phone rang about an hour later, and she quickly picked up the receiver to be greeted by Mark.

Dorothy began to tremble as she asked him if he and Eden were okay. His reply stunned her.

"We are at the City Hospital," he reported to Dorothy.

"What has been going on?" Dorothy demanded.

Mark's story left her speechless. He explained to the older woman that, while on a picnic in a cabin in the bush, Eden had begun to bleed and that she and Mark had been extremely concerned for her wellbeing, as well as for that of their baby.

Mark had endeavoured to lift himself out of his wheelchair in an effort to try to run for help but had been unable to make his legs work. As he and Eden had become increasingly distressed, Mark was at a complete loss as to how to get help for his wife and their baby. He then said something which sent 'holy chills' through Dorothy's entire being.

"Suddenly," Mark told the woman, "I felt an electricity of some type run through my entire body and a surge of power in my legs. Immediately, without thinking, I found myself on my feet and running from the cabin down the dirt track."

Dorothy gasped as Mark continued to speak.

"I stopped a van which was travelling past and, with the driver's assistance, we managed to get to the cabin and transport Eden to hospital."

Mark told Dorothy that Eden had been given some medicine to attempt to stop the bleeding. She had then been taken into the operating theatre for an emergency caesarian. The doctors had delivered dangerously premature twin girls who were, at this time, fighting like little troopers in the Paediatric Intensive Care Unit.

"Twins?" Dorothy responded in shock, wondering why the doctors had not been able to pick up that Eden was carrying two babies at an earlier stage.

"Yes," Mark replied. "We have named them Chellsey and Sasha, and they desperately need our prayers as they are fighting for their lives."

He told Dorothy that Eden was now recovering well and that he had left her for a few minutes to make this phone call to her.

"I have no idea of how I was able so suddenly to walk." Mark wept as he continued to fill Dorothy in on all that had happened.

Dorothy who was barely able to speak, began to tell Mark her story of the events which had unfolded at her home that afternoon and told Mark that she would leave for the hospital immediately. Both she and Mark were greatly rejoicing in the knowledge that God had performed a mighty miracle that day.

Meanwhile, Fred was extremely worried to find that neither Eden nor Mark were there when he returned to collect them from the cabin. Even more puzzling to him was the fact that Mark's wheelchair was sitting there unoccupied and that the food for their picnic was untouched. It was then that he noticed the blood which was covering parts of the floor in large patches.

Very concerned at this, he quickly jumped back into the couple's vehicle and headed for their home where, of course, he also found no sign of Mark and Eden.

He then dialled the phone number of the town's Medical Centre but they were unable to shed any light upon the situation.

Finally, he made a phone call to West End City Hospital, and was informed that Eden Hanson was an inpatient in their maternity ward.

"What about Mark?" he wondered, while feeling concern for Eden. He was unable to understand why Mark's wheelchair had been left in the cabin while he himself was not there. With many questions swirling around in his mind, he headed for the hospital in the hope of at least being able to talk with his patient, assuming that he was there.

He desperately wanted the mysterious circumstances, which he had encountered at the cabin, explained.

Upon her arrival at the hospital, Dorothy Moore headed for the maternity ward and easily located Eden who was resting in a private room. She looked up as Dorothy entered the room and smiled weakly, pleased to see her friend. Dorothy walked over to the bed and embraced Eden, asking where Mark was. Eden told her that he had gone to visit their daughters. Dorothy told Eden that Mark had unfolded the series of events that day to her, including the incredible fact that he was once more able to walk.

Eden broke into a grin and agreed with her friend that God had been so very good to the couple.

She was, however, concerned for their baby daughters, both of whom were very weak and in need of critical care. Dorothy replied, telling Eden that she had not ceased to pray for the babies, as well as for her and Mark, from the time she had heard the incredulous story a little earlier, when Mark had phoned her to explain all that had taken place during the afternoon.

At that moment, Mark entered the room in tears. He briefly acknowledged Dorothy before bending over his wife and stroking her hair. "I'm sorry to have to tell you, sweetheart, that Sasha passed away a few minutes ago. Her lungs were just too weak," he softly told the two women before doing his best to comfort his wife who had broken down with grief at this news.

Mark continued to speak, telling them that the doctors were optimistic that Chellsey would survive as she was the larger and the stronger of the twins.

Dorothy also wept with the couple and promised to pray for little Chellsey to pull through.

Eden sighed and then yawned. It was obvious that she was exhausted, as well as understandably upset about the death of her and Mark's daughter. Admitting that she needed some 'alone time', she suggested that Mark take Dorothy down to show her their baby, while she tried to rest.

Mark and Dorothy agreed, and left the room heading for the Paediatric Intensive Care Unit.

Mark remarked that Eden and he would need to arrange a small burial service for Sasha. However, he told Dorothy that it was best for Eden to rest right now. Dorothy agreed and took Mark's arm as they headed to the I.C.U ward, both fighting back tears over Sasha's death.

Fred finally arrived at the hospital after having to stop en route to fix a punctured tyre in the vehicle. He found that the door to Eden's room was closed and could not hear any voices coming from within. He decided to wait for a while in the ward's visitors' lounge. He was hoping that Mark and Eden were okay and he sat with some impatience in one of the lounge's easy chairs, hoping to catch sight of Mark or Eden.

Mark and Dorothy passed the visitors' room on their way back to say their goodbyes to Eden.

The nurses had told them she needed to rest.

Fred caught sight of them and was speechless to see that Mark was walking and seemed to be doing so without any problem. He called to Mark who entered the lounge, smiling. Answering the questions in Fred's eyes, he said that he had an incredible story to tell his carer.

"I can see that," Fred replied.

Mark told Fred that he would give him a thorough rundown of the happenings of the afternoon as the two drove home.

Fred was absolutely stunned to see Mark up and on his feet, and the two men walked in silence to Mark and Eden's vehicle. Mark held out his hand for the keys, telling Fred that he would drive the pair home. They both then jumped into the car with Mark behind the wheel and Fred still in shock, unable to think of any plausible reason that Mark could possibly be back on his feet.

As the two men headed for home with Mark behind the wheel, he began to recount to Fred the astonishing events which had taken place that afternoon.

THE END